BIGGEST LITTLE SECRET

BOBBY HUTCHINSON

SUNFLOWER PUBLISHING

FOREWORD

Starwood is a little coal mining town deep in the Canadian Rockies where romance flourishes, intrigue abounds and lives are never as simple as they seem.

Starwood is the setting for **Starwood Chronicles**, a series of short exciting reads about the fun people who lead their lives in the shadow of the Rocky Mountains.

The first four in the series are:

BIGGEST LITTLE TRUCKSTOP

EVERY LITTLE THING

BIGGEST LITTLE MUSTACHE

BIGGEST LITTLE HEART

I hope you enjoy **Biggest Little Secret**

I'd be so grateful for a review on Amazon.

I'd also like to give you a free book, one from another series , DOCTOR 911, stories about doctors and hospitals, life and death—and, of course, love. You can get it here:

ARE YOU
My DADDY?
BOBBY
HUTCHINSON
Medical Romance, Emergency Series

1

———

Harper Goodman stumbled off of Baxter's Shuttle Service in Starwood and pulled the blue billed cap down further over her ginger hair, wincing when she raised her arm. She dug her cell phone out and tapped in Joanne's number, weak with relief when her friend answered.

"J-bird, I need a huge favor." Harper's voice echoed through the receiver. She knew she sounded strange. "I'm at the Starwood Bus Station. Do you think you could come pick me up?" Her voice cracked, and tears streamed down her cheeks when Joanne said, "Of course. Sit tight. We'll be there in a few minutes."

Harper's stomach, already uneasy, clenched. She fought against the nausea that threatened to gag her as she painfully shouldered her back pack and waited while the bus driver unloaded her fat blue suitcase. She shoved her dark glasses further up her nose, mopped at her cheeks with her hand and then absently rubbed her aching shoulder.

"Welcome to Starwood," the skinny driver smiled. He had bad teeth. There was something smarmy about him. "I hear it's a real friendly little place. You coming here to work? I hear the mines are hiring lots of new people."

"I'm not staying," she snapped, grabbing her bag and turning away. He'd tried to start up a conversation at every stop between here and Calgary, where she'd gotten on. He gave her the creeps, but so did almost every guy she saw these days.

She didn't trust him. She didn't trust *anyone*. He might know Brad, he could be reporting back to the violent man from whom she was trying desperately to escape. Her heart hammered and she felt dizzy with sudden panic. Her eyes, behind her dark glasses, swung right and then left, searching.

What if Brad was here already? What if—she let out a muffled scream and stumbled back when someone put a hand on her arm.

"Hey, easy does it, it's just me." Joanne gave her a hug and then took Harper's suitcase. "The car's right over here, c'mon."

Harper fell into Joanne's arms, sobbing.

The dark glasses slipped off and Joanne grabbed them and tucked them in her jacket pocket. She wrapped her arms around her oldest friend and let Harper cry for as long as she needed.

"What happened?" she asked once Harper quieted.

"I need help," Harper croaked. "Oh, J-bird, I'm in bad trouble."

Joanne reached over, tracing the outline of the bruise around Harper's left eye, brushing away the new tears that were streaming down her face.

"You've come to the right place," Joanne said quietly. "Let's go, and you can tell me all about it."

Joanne picked up the suitcase, her arm protectively around her friend.

Harper looked around to see who might have been watching.

The bus driver, standing by the door of the small depot, waved at her, and she shuddered.

"The car's right over here, c'mon, love."

They'd almost made it when a tall guy wearing workman's coveralls called from across the street, "Joanne? Hey, Joanne, about those steps at the daycare—"

He came hurrying towards them. Light brown hair, the hint of a beard, he was probably six-four with shoulders and arms that signaled hard physical work. He had strong features, dark eyes, long eyelashes—and he was staring at her.

Harper gasped, certain that he was one of Brad's lackeys, come to let her know that she couldn't hide.

"It's okay, he's my friend," Joanne whispered, turning to greet him with a smile.

"Hey Quinn, how you doing? This is my friend Harper Goodman. Harper, Quinn Valdez. Quinn's the finest carpenter around, he built the deck on my house and somehow managed to install a second bathroom."

Harper's heart was hammering. She couldn't be sure of anything, but Joanne knew the guy. Maybe he was alright? But--maybe not?

She managed a nod and mumbled, "Joanne, could we just go---?"

"Of course. Quinn, drop around tomorrow, would you? Then we can figure out what needs to be done."

The guy gave Harper a quizzical look. "Pleased to meet you, Harper." His voice was deep and warm and sort of comforting. "Sure, Joanne, I'll come by. Morning or afternoon?"

"Come for lunch, why don't you? The kids would love to see you."

He gave them both a wide, engaging grin and with a small salute he turned away.

It wasn't until they were safely inside the car and driving away that some of the tension left Harper's body.

"I didn't want your kids to see me like this," Harper said in a voice so small it was barely even audible to herself. "Where are they?"

She dreaded meeting the kids. She'd been steeling herself ever since Joanne answered her desperate phone call.

"It's okay, the kids aren't even here. Colin's taken them out for a picnic, so we can have a few moments alone. And once we explain that you had an accident but you're fine, they'll accept it."

It was a relief not to have to meet them yet. Maybe she could get her emotions in check before it happened. Harper blew her nose, her mind going back to the man Joanne had introduced. "You know this Quinn guy well? Has he been around a long time, or just lately?"

"Quinn? He was born here, he left to join the army for a few years. But he had a handicapped sister, Lucy, and after his mother died, he came back to care for her. Lucy passed on a year ago. Quinn took it really hard. He's a great guy."

"I just thought—I was scared that—maybe he might—"

"Oh, Harper, I'm so sorry. I didn't understand quite how terrified you must feel. But you don't have to be afraid here in Starwood." Joanne glanced over at her and winced at the purple bruises and swollen eyelids. "I take it Brad did that," she said, anger in her voice.

Harper didn't answer. She didn't have to. Joanne knew what Brad was capable of.

After a few moments Joanne pulled into a parking spot in front of a cute little two-storey house and parked, but Harper didn't move out of her seat.

"Sweetie, what's wrong?" Joanne asked. "You're safe here, I promise you that."

"I'm so afraid I'll bring trouble down on you. If Brad finds out where I am—"

"Stop this now. I'm not afraid of Brad, and Colin certainly isn't. And anyhow, there's no way he's going to find you, Harper." Joanne got out and came over to the passenger door. "C'mon inside, I'll make us a cup of tea."

"I've ruined your day," Harper looked into Joanne's kind hazel eyes, tears burning at the corners of her own. "You were all planning a picnic, weren't you?"

"Nonsense, you haven't ruined anything," Joanne ran a caring hand down Harper's arm. "I love that you're here. Come on, let's get you settled inside."

Harper studied the kitchen, the living room, and the small playroom on the main floor.

The fastest way out of the house from the kitchen was through the window of the laundry room, that took you straight to the backyard. The playroom window was tiny, but she figured she could fit through it.

It wasn't that Harper didn't trust Joanne. She wouldn't be here if she didn't. But things could turn sour in a moment's notice, and she needed to be ready.

Joanne lived in Starwood, which was only a two-and-a-half-hour drive from Calgary. That meant she was only hours away from Brad, which wasn't remotely far enough. Maybe there was nowhere far enough. The thought made her want to run and never stop.

"Tea?" Joanne offered, putting the kettle on, after she'd helped Harper into a chair. Her muscles were stiffening up, the bruises aching. There was a sharp pain in her ribs every time she tried to take a deep breath.

She felt eighty years old instead of thirty-nine.

"You got anything stronger than tea?" Harper asked.

Joanne looked over at her with her eyebrows slightly raised, and Harper forced a smile. "Okay, okay, tea is fine." Owning the Whiskey-Jack Pub had made relying on liquor way too easy. Maybe it was past time to switch to tea. She'd been drinking far too much the last while.

Joanne poured them each a cup and then took a seat right next to Harper, studying her. "You've lost at least ten pounds since I last saw you, girl. Slender is okay, but you're taking it to skinny." She studied Harper's face, her mouth tight and her eyes horrified as she tenderly lifted aside the cotton turtleneck and then tugged the long sleeves above the elbow.

Harper knew there were bruises everywhere. She winced as Joanne drew up the cotton sweater and swore under her breath at the sight of Harper's ribs.

"Harper, are your ribs broken? Do you have internal injuries? I think you need to see a doctor," Joanne said.

"Do you have anyone particular in mind?" Harper tried to lighten the mood, knowing that Joanne had recently married a doctor. "Perhaps a handsome fellow with an Irish brogue named Colin?"

"I'm serious, Harper. These bruises look really bad. You might be bleeding internally."

"I'm fine, J-bird," Harper reached over and took Joanne's hand into hers. "I'm fine now that I'm here with you."

Joanne shook her head. "I'm really worried about you, my lovely friend."

Harper shrugged. "Not the first time I got smacked around, maybe not the last. Although I hope to God it is. I'm getting too old for this." She remembered the older girl, Maddie, who'd first taught her how to get out of the way when foster parents became abusive.

"*Hide,*" Maddie had advised. "*Always scope out a hiding place, keep an emergency bag packed. And look for the fastest way out of the house the very first time you go through the front door.*"

Harper had passed on that valuable advice to all the other foster kids she encountered. If the kids weren't going to get love and care from the people that were responsible for giving them just that, then they needed to give one another all the help and information and affection they could.

No matter how much you were hurting, you never gave up on the other kids. You never ratted them out, you did what you could for them.

She'd drilled those rules into all those kids. But then she forgot her own rules with Brad. Well, she wasn't about to ever again.

"You took such good care of me. You warned me about Brad and I didn't listen. And then, when I had the abortion-" Joanne gulped, her eyes filling with tears behind her red glasses. "You saved my life, Harper. Now I want to return the favor. What happened?" Joanne gently squeezed her hand.

"Brad happened," Harper said simply.

Joanne nodded and then shifted around in the chair. "I got that. But why? I know you said he was helping you out financially with the pub, but why on earth---?"

"It doesn't matter," Harper waved her hand dismissively. "I got sucked in. I fell for his garbage. And then I double crossed him. It's not like it takes a lot to get him mad." She let out a little puff of air and dropped her eyes to the table.

Joanne had sounded so happy on the phone when Harper called her, and now she felt horrible for messing with that happiness. She'd been desperate, hurting and scared. She hadn't known anyone else to call. And there was also the secret she'd been packing around so long. It was like a bag of rocks that got heavier all the time.

But she was sorry now for being so weak.

She knew all too well that Joanne had a family. And Harper could be putting all of them in danger by coming here.

"Did it--was it because of what happened with me?" Joanne asked. "Because I made that appointment to see him that time, to borrow money from him? And then changed my mind?"

Harper shook her head but didn't reply. Neither did she meet Joanne's eyes.

"'Because I've been calling to thank you for stopping me from going to Brad for help, for money to bribe that doctor, so Zalika could stay in Canada. But you never picked up. I should have driven back to Calgary to check up on you. I am so sorry, Harper." Joanne pushed her glasses aside and mopped at her eyes with a tissue.

Harper shook her head. She'd avoided Joanne's calls. She'd needed to come to a decision on her own. "Please don't apologize. And omigod, don't cry, you'll get me started." She put her hand on Joanne's forearm. "This was *not* your fault. I did other things, things that Brad found out about and got pissed."

"I still should have made sure you were alright," Joanne put her own hand on top of Harper's. "I'm here for you now.

Whatever you need." Joanne leaned over and carefully hugged her friend.

"I know, and I'm so grateful." Bone weary, Harper laid her head on Joanne's shoulder. "For now, I'm just exhausted," she sighed.

"I'll get the bedroom ready for you, I'll just change the sheets." Joanne shot off the chair.

"I have enough to get a room at the hotel if-"

"Don't be ridiculous, of course you're staying here. Just give me a few minutes," she smiled.

Harper slowly got off the chair and wandered around the house, cup of tea cradled in her hands. Her ribs hurt a little less if she wasn't sitting. She went into the living room and looked at the dozens of framed pictures scattered around the place. They were on the fireplace mantel and the side table, even on the bookshelf.

Kids. Joanne and Colin's wedding picture.

Harper studied it. Colin looked salt of the earth, lovely blue eyes, dark curls spilling over his shirt collar. A good, decent man.

Joanne had told her that the marriage at first was one of convenience, just to keep Zalika in the country, to renew her Visa. But it had become something so much more. He loved the three foster kids, and he loved Joanne. The expression on their faces spelled out the truth; their marriage was a real one.

Harper was pleased for Joanne.

And here was Joanne cradling her three foster kids in her arms, brown haired Alex, dark little Zalika, and Lily.

Harper's eyes lingered on the delicate four-year-old. She had huge hazel eyes, brownish blonde hair that seemed kissed with sunshine. And that crooked, endearing grin. Harper reached out a finger and traced the girl's face, and then she tore her gaze away, breathing shallow because of the pain in her ribs—and in her heart.

She wanted to lay all the photos flat so the images didn't show. Instead she studied the books, which were filed in alphabetical order. Joanne always did have a sense of order; years ago, when she worked with Harper waitressing, it was always Joanne who kept track of the tips, making sure they got their fair share.

She took one book off the shelf and turned it around to look at the cover, and her heart sank. It was the silhouette of a woman and a child walking at the beach at sunset, holding hands. Trembling, she shoved it back and picked up another one. A woman in Amish clothing, sitting on a rocking chair, holding a pair of baby shoes. She laid that one face down on the table.

"Feel free to borrow anything you like," Joanne said from behind her, making her jump. "Though most of them are textbooks I used when I was at school, taking the early education course I needed to open the daycare."

"Thanks." Harper shook her head, forcing a smile. "I'm not much of a reader anymore." She did her best to sound ultra-casual. "How's it going with the adoptions? Any more news on Zalika?"

"Zalika's Visa was renewed, and we've applied to adopt. It's just a matter of paperwork since she was an orphan. Lily's adoption should go through next month, we're over-joyed about it, and so is she." Joanne's face clouded. "But there's a problem with Alex. His birth mother won't release him for adoption."

"Do you know why?" Harper's gaze went to the photo of Joanne and her babies.

Joanne shook her head. "We know something about Lily,

who her birth mother is. But with Alex the records are sealed, so we have no idea at all."

"Maybe she'll change her mind."

"That would be a miracle. Keep your fingers crossed for us. Now, your room's ready, come on," Joanne hooked an arm around Harper's waist. They climbed the stairs slowly, one by one, and then stopped in front of the second room to the right. There were bunk beds, one with a Superman spread, the other in pastel pink.

"Master bedroom's down the hall, Lily and Alex sleep in here. We still have Zalika in with us. With the heart problems she's had, I feel better keeping her close at night. The bathroom's here and here's your room. Sorry it's so small." She led the way to a tiny room barely big enough for the single bed and small dresser it held.

"It's about the size of a closet," Joanne apologized. "I hope you'll be comfortable, at least the bed's got a good mattress."

"It's perfect. I can't thank you enough, J-bird." Harper was relieved to see that the tiny room had a fair-sized window. She walked over and estimated the drop to the ground. "Thank you for doing this for me."

"Promise you'll let Colin have a look at those bruises later on."

"They're fine, honest. Don't even hurt," Harper lied.

Joanne raised her eyebrows. "Please, Harper? Just to put my mind at ease," she pleaded.

"Okay, okay. You're such a fuss pot, J-bird." Gingerly, Harper sank down on the bed. She felt as though her legs wouldn't carry her much further. Her insides were trembling. She took off her billed cap and put it on the chair by the bed.

Joanne touched a fond hand to Harper's gingery hair.

"You get some rest now. I'll be downstairs if you need me."
She smiled and closed the door.

Harper struggled up to use the bathroom. When she
came back, she turned the old-fashioned key that was in the
lock on her door. She hated upstairs rooms. The escape
routes were a lot more complicated, but this one was not
that high off the ground. She'd survive the drop.

She kicked off her shoes and fell on the bed, completely
exhausted. The bruise on her ribs hurt like hell, made her
nauseous.

Maybe Joanne was right and she needed to have it
looked at. But she didn't want it to be Colin. Not Joanne's
husband.

Because then he'd see the scar low down on her
abdomen and he'd know right away. And she couldn't risk
that.

2

Harper woke with a start to a dark room, a silent, sleeping house.

The clock beside the bed said five-forty A.M.

She sat up with difficulty, unable to believe she'd slept through the previous evening and the entire night. She wasn't usually a heavy sleeper, but she'd been awake and in hiding for forty-eight hours in Calgary. What day was it? She checked her cell.

Saturday. October 14th. Somehow, she'd lost several days.

She listened closely through the door, for any signs that someone else might be awake. There was nothing but silence.

She needed the toilet. She unlocked the door and slipped into the bathroom. She had a quick shower and was tiptoeing back to her room when a tiny sound caught her attention.

Right opposite the bathroom was the kid's bedroom. The door was half-open and a small girl was standing there with one thumb in her mouth, a teddy bear pressed hard against her side, her thick blonde curls tousled.

Lily removed the thumb, grinned and waved shyly at Harper. Then she turned around and hurried back into her room, closing the door slowly behind her, watching Harper until the final click sounded.

Harper's breath caught. Slowly she went back into her room and sat down heavily on the edge of her bed. It had been such a huge mistake to come here. She'd have to leave as soon as she possibly could. She heard a deep male voice and kid's voices responding. Then there was a clatter on the stairs, and then Joanne's giggle.

She had to muster all of her courage to go downstairs once she knew that everyone was up. She'd tried to cover up the bruises under her eyes with some makeup, but it was a futile effort. Her pale skin showed every mark, including the freckles on her nose and cheeks.

She'd shampooed her thick hair and brushed it out loose, hoping it would hide some of the bruising on her neck. And Joanne was right, she'd gotten downright skinny. Her jeans, which had been skin tight, now hung loose on her hips and waist. And her cheekbones stood out like blades on her face. Her green eyes were rimmed with even darker inky bruises this morning. She put a tentative finger on the bridge of her nose. She'd thought he'd broken it, but maybe not. There was nothing more she could do about it, so she took a deep breath and headed downstairs.

They were all seated around the kitchen table.

"Harper, good morning, love," Joanne leaped off her chair. She rushed to her and gave her a huge hug. "I'm so glad you had a long sleep, I tapped at your door last night because I thought you'd be hungry, but you must have been out of it. And you have to be starving by now, there's yogurt and hot cereal and boiled eggs and toast. I'll get you some coffee. Kids, this is Auntie Harper. She'll be staying with us a while."

Harper tried for a smile, raised her hand and gave them an awkward wave as Joanne introduced her family.

"This tiny human is Zalika, that is lovely Lily and the big guy's name is Alex," Joanne said. Her face was suffused with pride and her voice betrayed her when she said, "And of course, my husband, Colin." He got up and walked over to Harper, a warm smile on his rugged face.

"Truly great to finally meet you, Harper," he took her hand between both of his, his Irish brogue charming.

"You too, Colin." Harper smiled but avoided his gaze, knowing he was assessing the bruises.

"Come, sit, have some breakfast." Joanne pointed at the spot they had already set up for her. She poured a steaming mugful of coffee and handed it over.

"Thanks," Harper sat down and filled her plate. She *was* starving. After her first couple of bites, however, she stopped. She felt two sets of small, inquisitive eyes watching her closely. She looked around the table. The baby was being fed by Colin and was completely uninterested in her. The other two kids had their eyes fixed on her.

"How did you get an ouchie, Auntie?" Alex inquired.

"Auntie Harper fell down some stairs," Joanne was quick to answer.

Harper didn't speak. If it was left to her, she wouldn't have lied. The sooner they learned there are more bad people in the world than good, the better they'd be able to protect themselves, learn not to trust everyone.

But Joanne's explanation seemed to satisfy the little boy enough for him to get back to his breakfast without any further questions.

Lily was still quietly staring at her. "I saw you before," she said, nodding her head. "You got's orange hair."

"I'm afraid I do," Harper agreed. She cleared her throat and tried for nonchalance. "I guess that last coloring job went sadly wrong." She was so relieved the little girl hadn't mentioned her black eyes.

"Auntie's fooling us, she doesn't color her hair," Joanne said. "It's always been that beautiful mix of brown and gold and red."

Colin got up from the table and kissed Joanne and then each of the kids. "Sorry, everyone, I know it's Saturday, but I have a very ill patient to visit this morning. I'll see you all later." He turned to Harper. "Joanne says you need to see me, please get her to call and I'll wait for you at the office if you like."

"Thanks," Harper lied, knowing she wasn't about to do any such thing. She couldn't set one foot outside this house in case someone dangerous saw her and reported back to Brad.

When Colin left, Joanne re-filled her own coffee cup and sat down. She pointed at Harper's plate. "You haven't eaten more than a bite. I'll just sit here until you do."

Harper whispered to Alex, "Does she do this to you guys?"

"Yup. We gotta eat so we can grow, Mama says." He was a solemn little boy with huge intelligent eyes. Harper thought about the adoption problem, about his mother not releasing him. Her heart began to hammer in her chest.

"Harper, you must eat." Joanne was adamant.

Dutifully, Harper made an attempt to finish the food on her plate, but her stomach was upset.

Joanne refilled their coffee cups, and it was a relief when the kids went off to play.

"Harper, have you thought of reporting Brad to the cops? The local Staff Sergeant, Luke Philips, is a good friend. I really trust him. I could—"

"No." Harper shook her head and sprang up from the table, wincing when her ribs screamed an objection. "J-bird, please, no, don't say a word to the cops. Brad would—he'll kill me, I swear he will."

"But Harper, what are you going to do? You own the Whiskey Jack, you can't just walk away from that, it's your livelihood. And you can't live your life in fear of that—that monster."

Harper knew that all of what Joanne was saying was true. She'd left Sweeney, a long-time employee, running the pub, but he wasn't familiar with stock control or how much maintenance was required. And she loved running the Whiskey-Jack. When she bought it five years ago, she'd had plans to start serving food, to upgrade and attract a whole different clientele. Except that she'd had to borrow money from Brad to buy the place. And that marked the end of her dreams.

So now she owed him, and he'd tacked on exorbitant interest to the original loan. She'd never gotten ahead financially enough to make any changes, so the place was the same old dive bar.

"Harper," Joanne said. "Why exactly is Brad after you?"

"He's trafficking women and drugs and using the Whiskey-Jack as a front," she said in an even tone. "A while ago I started using whatever money I could spare to help the girls get out and to get them as far away from Calgary as possible. I cost him a lot of money and business. And he found out," she explained. This was the first time she had said all that out loud. It felt both liberating and nauseating.

Joanne leaned over and took Harper's hands in hers.

"You are so brave for helping those women," she said. "I know how much courage that takes. And now you need to help yourself too and give him up."

"I can't. Others have tried, but he's just too powerful." Her voice quavered. "I don't see how I'm going to get out of this." There was so much more to it than Joanne realized. So much more that no one else knew.

"I don't believe there's only one solution when things are desperate, my friend," Joanne said in a firm voice. "You stopped me from borrowing money from Brad and that resulted in me marrying Colin. It was a marriage of convenience at first, to keep Zalika safe. But Harper, it was a miracle because we totally love one another. I'm happier than I've ever been, and that's because of you. You helped me. Please, can you trust Colin and I to help you?"

Harper stared into her friend's lovely heart shaped face, into the kind eyes behind the big red glasses and guilt rose up to consume her.

There were things Joanne didn't know, things that Harper could never tell her, no matter how much she needed someone to confide in.

She really should grab her bags and leave. But she'd pretty much run out of energy and options. She was bone weary, so tired of being afraid, of feeling she was trapped in a maze of deceit and debt and lies and danger. Every inch of her body hurt. She had no energy left for anything, not even running.

"Let me think about it," she sighed, knowing she'd never give in.

"Good enough." Joanne got up and began clearing the table. "Now you just rest today, stretch out over there on the sofa and relax."

Harper thought of protesting, but she hurt too badly to

argue. And she felt strangely safe here. She did as Joanne suggested, and her friend shoved a pillow under her head and covered her with a cloud soft blue afghan. She wouldn't sleep, she'd just rest a little—

She had no idea how long it had been before she was startled awake at the sound of a man's deep voice in the entrance hall, and she sat up too quickly and then gasped at the pain in her ribs.

Before she could bolt for the stairs, Joanne came into the room with the tall man she'd introduced Harper to the day before.

Trapped, Harper hung her head, rubbing the sleep from her eyes, wishing she was anywhere but there.

"Good, you're awake." Joanne put a hand on the man's arm. "Harper, you remember Quinn Valdez?"

"Hi again, Harper." Quinn nodded to her. A pair of very dark eyes looked down at her. His mouth had smile lines around it.

Harper shoved her hair out of her eyes. "Sorry, I guess I fell asleep." She got to her feet, wincing at the pain in her ribs. "If you'll excuse me, I'll just—" She headed for the stairs, intending to hide in her room. She remembered now that Joanne had invited this Quinn guy to lunch.

"Don't be long, lunch is all ready," Joanne called after her, and at first, Harper was annoyed at Joanne for trying to force her to come down again. But then she realized she actually was hungry.

She used the bathroom, splashed her face with cold water, brushed her hair and dotted more makeup under her eyes, not that it helped. She hesitated at the top of the stairs, but the smell of homemade soup and grilled cheese lured her down.

Quinn was already seated at the kitchen table, but he got

to his feet when Harper appeared, holding the chair right beside him for her to sit down. She couldn't help but notice the way his tee shirt fit across amazingly broad shoulders, the way his dark jeans hung low, but not too low, on his lean hips.

There were only three places set at the table.

"Where are the kids? And Colin?" Harper sat, trying not to grimace at the pain in her ribs.

"Colin said he'd try to make it for lunch, but there was an accident on one of the farms up the Valley. He won't be home till later this afternoon. And I fed the gang earlier, they're down for naps." Joanne was serving blue china bowls of wonderful smelling soup, setting a platter of grilled cheese and tomato sandwiches in the centre of the table.

Harper's mouth watered at the wonderful smells. She was all too conscious of Quinn's muscular arm nearly touching her own and she moved away.

"Great food, Joanne." Quinn ate with a healthy man's appetite, and Harper also spooned up the thick squash soup and devoured her grilled cheese sandwich.

Joanne and Quinn chatted like old friends, but Harper stayed quiet.

She shot glances at Quinn. He wasn't as young as she'd first thought. He had lines beside his dark eyes, at the corners of his wide mouth. He had muscles in his thighs that weren't disguised by the slim jeans. Large hands, square fingers, evenly cut nails. She shivered. He could be dangerous. He made her nervous. As soon as she was done, she planned to head up to her room and leave Joanne and Quinn alone to discuss their business.

But half way through the meal Zalika started wailing upstairs and Joanne hurried off to tend to her.

Harper didn't look at Quinn, but she could feel him studying her.

"I feel like I know you from somewhere," he said.

Every muscle in Harper's body tensed. "I don't think so," she managed to say.

"You're from Calgary, right? You run a bar there, don't you? The Whiskey-Jack?"

Harper felt all the blood drain from her face. She felt dizzy.

"Couple of buddies of mine are regulars there," he added. "I went with them one night and they pointed you out. You beat them at pool a couple times, they were impressed."

"So—so you and your friend's know Brad?" It was all she could do not to run. But all her things were upstairs, she had no money on her. She should have remembered not ever to be more than a few feet away from her purse.

Quinn frowned. "Brad? Brad who?"

"Brad Blackwell." It was all she could do to choke out the name.

He shook his head and shrugged. "Never met the dude, sorry." He studied her and something slowly changed in his expression. "Is he the one who beat the crap out of you?" There was an undercurrent of anger and something else in his deep soothing voice, something like concern.

Harper was frozen with fear. She tried to pick up her water glass, but her hand shook so much it slopped over.

He stared at her. "My god, you're scared of *me*. Harper, I swear I never met this Brad asshole." His voice deepened. "Although I wouldn't mind giving him some of his own medicine." He reached out a finger to touch her bruised wrist, but she jerked her arm back.

There was something so straightforward about him. "I

don't—please, you can't—he doesn't know where I am. He *can't* know that I'm here. Please, he could—he *would*, he *will* cause—cause trouble for Joanne. For—for her family." She knew she was begging. She couldn't stop herself. "He can't find me, he just can't."

"And that's exactly how it'll stay. I promise you, Harper, I would never bring trouble on you, or on Joanne or Colin." His voice was a low growl. "I won't say a word to anyone about you being here. You have my word on that." He leaned towards her. "With one condition."

Here it came. There were always conditions. They always cost her dearly. She waited, wondering if her lunch was going to come back up.

"You program my number into your cell, as an emergency number, so you only have to touch it once to reach me. If there's one hint of trouble, even if you're just scared, you call me. Anytime, day or night. You keep your cell with you every minute. Starwood's not big, I can be with you in a matter of minutes."

She swallowed hard, staring at him. "Why—why would you want that? Why would you do that for—for *me*? I don't even know you."

He held her gaze and then he looked away. "I grew up in an abusive household. My father beat my mother. He died, fortunately, when I was ten. My little sister was three."

It was a scenario she knew a lot about. Foster homes weren't immune to domestic violence, at least not the ones she'd been in.

"I have no use for men who beat on women. It's a foible of mine." There was quiet menace in his tone.

"I'm sorry. About your mother, Quinn. And your sister. Joanne told me." It was the first time she'd used his name and he noticed.

"Thank you, Harper." He smiled at her, a wide, white open smile that brought some warmth back to her body. "Where's your cell?"

She dug it out of her pocket and handed it to him.

He typed in his number and gave it back.

She stuck it in the pocket of her jeans and felt a tiny bit of the terrible fear release its hold on her.

Joanne came back just then, and the conversation turned to repairs on the stairs leading down to the area she rented from the library for her daycare.

Harper cleared the table and loaded the dishwasher.

Details for the repairs settled, Quinn thanked Joanne for lunch and got up to leave. He came over to Harper and took her hand in both of his. His grip was gentle.

"A real pleasure talking with you, Harper. I'll stay in touch. Remember what I told you." He winked at her, and to her amazement she felt herself blushing. What was with that? She'd swear she hadn't blushed in years. And, of course, Joanne noticed.

When he was gone, she raised her eyebrows and grinned at Harper. "So, you and Quinn got friendly," she teased. "I'm so glad, he's a great guy. He's single, too. Apparently, he was married once for a short time, but it didn't work out. She wasn't from around here, and she dumped him when he came back to care for his sister."

"He's okay. Too bad I didn't meet a decent man like him a long time ago."

"It's never too late, look at me and Colin."

But it was too late for her, Harper told herself. She had way too much baggage to even think of having any sort of relationship. And bashed up as she was, how could a guy like that want anything to do with her?

The kids woke up and Joanne took them out for a walk

to the play-park. Harper sorted out her backpack and her suitcase. She'd thrown things in her bag in such a hurry she had no idea what she'd actually brought. She needed it in order if she should have to leave fast. She was sorting through and folding when she heard the front door open and close.

Her heart gave a thump, and she crept to the top of the stairs.

Colin was setting down his doctor's bag and shrugging out of his jacket. He glanced up and saw her. "Hey, Harper. Where's that wee wife of mine?"

"She took the kids out to the play-park just a few minutes ago." Her voice wobbled.

"And are you alright, then?" Colin sounded concerned.

"Yes, I just thought...I'm fine," Harper pressed her palm hard on her chest, trying to get her breathing under control. She slowly made her way down the stairs.

"Fine's not the way it looks, lass. Well, and isn't this just a good time to let me take a wee look at your ribs. Joanne thought you might have some broken."

Harper shook her head and held on to the edge of her shirt, pulling it down. "I—there's no need, it's just bruises."

Colin shook his head. "Joanne will scalp me bald unless I have a look at you. If I can tell her that I checked on you and you're fine, that'll earn me brownie points."

"You can lie and say you did," she offered in a weak voice.

"We don't do that, Jo and I," he said with a head-shake and a smile.

"Must be nice," Harper breathed.

"Come now, lass, I'll be gentle as a pediatric surgeon." He smiled. "Which I am, so you're in good hands."

"Well, J-bird clearly didn't fall for you because of your

great flirting skills," she attempted to make things uncomfortable. Maybe that would get her out of this.

He shook his head. "I wasn't flirting just now, but you're right. She didn't," he countered without missing one beat. "I have no skills whatsoever in that department. But I am a fine doctor, if I do say so myself."

"There's no way of getting out of this, is there?"

Colin shook his head. "I made a promise to Joanne. Just sit here on the table for a wee minute."

"Fine." There was no way out except to make a scene. She hoisted her bum on the table and lifted her shirt to reveal her ribs. The bruise looked even worse than yesterday. It felt worse too.

Colin was gently pressing around the dark purple area.

"Could you just please undo your jeans so that I can see how far down it goes?"

Harper *really* didn't want to. But she also wanted to just be done with this.

She closed her eyes while Colin examined her. The pain of the actual bruise was bad, but there was one spot that Colin touched that was agonizing. The bruising didn't go too far down, but with her pants open and pushed low around her hips, the scar from her C-section was clearly visible.

Colin, bless him, didn't comment except to say, "Okay lass, that'll do. All done."

Harper pulled up her pants and got off the table.

"You've a broken rib, maybe two, and deep bruising. You really should have some tests, an x-ray and a scan."

"No, please, Colin. I'll be leaving soon, there isn't time for tests." And she totally wasn't going anywhere public, like a hospital.

"Unless you rest up, the pains only going to get worse.

I'll give you some pain killers, but rest is what you really need. So, no talk of leaving, now. Just settle yourself and relax, let us care for you a little while."

"Colin, I'm afraid if I stay here your family's going to be in danger. You should be *kicking* me out!"

"Joanne would never do such a thing, and I'm not of a mind to either. We'll figure it out, the lot of us. Now you have a lay down on the sofa while I call out for pizza, it's our Saturday treat in this house. What toppings do ye fancy?"

His kindness was too much. The tears that trickled down Harper's cheeks had nothing to do with the pain in her body.

3

The huge crash pierced through the thick silence of the night, mixed with the sound of breaking glass, coming from somewhere else in the house, somewhere below her bedroom, on the main floor.

It tore Harper from a deep sleep, and she slid from the bed to the floor, instinctively seeking cover. She heard Colin's voice, children crying, the sound of his heavy footsteps racing downstairs, Joanne comforting the kids.

Harper got up, using the bed for leverage, her ribs white hot with pain. She unlocked her door and crept down the stairs, crouching on the last step.

It was in the living room. On the floor, among the broken window pieces, was a rock bathed in red paint.

Brad's signature threat. He'd used it on her before. Dizzy, terrified, Harper sank to the floor.

Colin had gone outside, and now he came back in, shaking his head.

"The bastard's long gone. I've called the police. Are you alright, Harper?"

"He talked," she whispered, her heart beating painfully hard in her chest. "Quinn. He told someone where I am."

Colin was saying something, but Harper couldn't hear him. There was a ringing in her ears. She could hear the blood rushing through her veins. Her jaw was clenched so hard that it hurt.

How could she ever have believed him, thought that she could trust him? She knew better than that. She had years of experience, seeing just how sincere they could look while lying straight through their teeth.

"You see why you should have let me leave? I need to go, right now."

"You're not going anywhere," Joanne, holding Zalika, was halfway down the stairs. The other two kids peered down at Harper and Colin.

Joanne came the rest of the way, helping Harper to her feet. Colin put his arms around his wife and the baby.

Harper bent over and touched the rock that was still dripping with paint. "This could have been thrown into one of your kids' rooms, I'm a danger to all of you."

Joanne handed the baby to Colin and then wrapped her arms around Harper.

"You asked for help," Joanne said softly into her ear. "So that's what we're doing. Harper, love. We're not about to abandon you just because some bully does this."

And Harper broke down. Joanne was only one of many friends from when she was younger. They got into a lot of trouble together. They had met Brad together. Joanne had gotten pregnant by him, had an abortion. And then she'd gotten out, got her life together, while Harper stayed behind and got in even deeper.

The things she'd done and had done to her since then were unspeakable. One particular thing was unforgivable.

Her other friends had fallen away, and yet here was Joanne, willing to stand by her side when no one else would.

And Colin, nodding, agreeing wholeheartedly with his wife.

"I don't deserve your help, J-bird."

"Don't you ever say that," Joanne held her close.

"If you—if you only knew...."

"I do know," Joanne said and smiled warmly when Harper looked at her with wide eyes. "I know some of it, maybe not all, but enough to know the fine woman you are. We'll get this sorted. Colin called Luke, he should be here in a minute to have a look at this and talk to you."

Harper started shaking her head.

"I know, I know, you don't trust the police. But Luke's just coming as a friend for now. Besides, he knows about Brad. From what happened with me, before. I told him and Colin exactly what Brad was, that day you stopped me from going to his house to borrow that money."

Luke Philips arrived within 20 minutes. He was wearing blue jeans and a checked shirt. He was tall, solid muscle, tousled black hair and icy blue eyes that bored into Harper, taking in the bruises, the careful way she moved.

For some reason Harper felt relieved he wasn't in uniform, although he was every inch RCMP as he searched outside around the house, took pictures on his phone, carefully bagged the rock.

When Philips was finally done, Joanne swept up the glass, vacuumed the last of the slivers, made strong coffee. She'd gotten the kids back to bed and asleep.

Colin and Luke hammered a piece of plywood over the gaping hole in the window, and then they all sat down at the table.

"Okay, Harper." Luke stirred cream and sugar into his

coffee mug, his disconcerting blue gaze on her. "Can you tell me what you think is going on here?"

She tried for a deep breath and winced when her broken ribs burned. There was no point anymore in hiding the truth. There was no way of hiding from Brad. He'd never stop coming after her.

She couldn't let herself think about Quinn and the way he'd betrayed her.

"I own a bar in Calgary, The Whiskey-Jack. I borrowed money from Brad Blackwell to buy it." She detailed the way he'd tricked her, promising to let her run the place her own way, then increasing the interest, using her premises for drug dealing and prostitution. She explained how she'd helped women who wanted to escape get away.

"You had a personal relationship with this man?" Luke's voice was neutral.

Harper grimaced and then nodded. "Off and on for several years. I tried to break away, but he figures women belong to him. He hardly ever let's go." She didn't look at Joanne.

"I was one of the lucky ones, I got away from him," Joanne said softly.

Colin reached over and took her hand in his.

Joanne's eyes brimmed with tears. "I was seventeen, pregnant with Brad's baby. He insisted I have an abortion. I let him bully me into it. Afterwards I knew what a huge mistake I'd made. I changed my life. He came after me, but I threatened to charge him with statutory rape. You helped me, Harper. I'll always be grateful for that. And then last year you and Colin kept me from asking him for a loan when I was terrified that Zalika would be sent back to Nigeria."

Harper looked over at Colin. His face was suffused with

love for Joanne. She thought of Quinn and his betrayal, and bile rose in her throat.

Luke asked for addresses, names of other people Brad had terrorized.

Harper shook her head. There were all the women she'd helped get away from him, but she'd never put them at risk by revealing their names. And anyway, she'd made sure she didn't know where they headed after she gave them money. It was an insurance policy, for her and for them.

"Do you have any idea how he found out where you're staying?"

"Yeah, I do." Harper's voice was bitter. "Quinn Valdez. He told Brad. He's been to the bar, he has friends who go there. He was here yesterday, he's the only person I've met here in Starwood."

Joanne gasped and shook her head, and Luke narrowed his eyes at Harper. "Valdez? You're quite sure of this?"

"Who else could it have been? I haven't left the house since I got here, no one else but him has come by."

"You're certain no one else knows that you're in Starwood, knows where you're staying?"

"I came on the shuttle bus. Joanne picked me up. The only person I've seen here apart from Colin and Joanne is Quinn."

"But we all know Quinn, he just wouldn't do something like this." Joanne turned to Luke. "You know him, Luke. You've known him a long time, it just doesn't make sense—"

"I'll speak to him. In the meantime, I'm posting an officer outside the house. Just in case." He glanced at his watch. "It's four in the morning, why don't you all try to get some sleep? There'll be someone watching, you can rest assured no one will bother you. Harper, I'll need you to come in to the station later in the morning and I'll take a formal statement. I'll have a squad car come by for you."

Luke left and there was a strained silence.

"I know Quinn's your friend," Harper sighed, feeling wretched. "I—I liked him. But who else could have done this? Who else--?"

There was a strained silence. "You guys have work in a few hours, you should try and get some rest. And so should I probably," Harper said. She was too shaken up to sleep, but she didn't want to inconvenience them any more than she already had. And she was accusing their friend, she could see that troubled both Joanne and Colin.

"Okay, we'll see you at breakfast," Joanne said. She and Colin went upstairs, hand in hand. Harper knew they were disturbed by her accusation of Quinn.

She walked over to the front window and stared at the police car parked outside. It made her feel safer than she thought it would. But the sense of betrayal she felt about Quinn made her nauseous.

He'd looked her straight in the eyes and sworn that he wasn't going to tell anyone. He'd even told her to call him if she felt threatened. She'd believed him, which was the worst part. She'd trusted him. And hadn't she vowed she wouldn't be taken in by a man ever again, after Brad?

And that same night Brad's people had found the house where she was staying.

She slowly climbed the stairs back to her room. She was about to lock her bedroom door when she heard the kid's door creak open.

Lily, sleep tousled and warm in her flannel gown, came towards Harper. She had her thumb in her mouth and she passed Harper and settled down on the bed, digging in under the duvet.

Harper looked at her, unsure what to do. "You alright, kid?"

The little girl nodded, snuggling in deeper.

"Want me to go get your mom?" Harper sat down on the edge of the bed.

Lily shook her head. "Come to bed wif' me, Auntie. I needs cuddles." She scooted closer to Harper, closed her eyes and went to sleep.

Harper stared down at the child. After a few moments, she carefully got up and went and tapped on Joanne's bedroom door, sticking her head in far enough to say that for some reason, Lily had chosen to sleep with her.

"Thanks for letting us know," Joanne said. "I'd have freaked, not finding her in her bunk."

Back in the bedroom, Harper crawled carefully into bed, drawing Lily into her arms, settling her against her own body.

For the first time in as long as she could remember, she murmured a heartfelt prayer. "Let me do the right thing," she repeated over and over. Please give me strength to do the right thing."

She finally slept, part of her ever conscious of the precious little girl she held in her arms.

At six thirty, Joanne came in. "Sorry, you two bedbugs, time for Lily to get up. Harper, you sleep as long as you can."

Lily threw herself into her mother's arms, grinning at Harper over her mother's shoulder, as though they'd shared a lovely joke.

Harper struggled out of bed. She needed to leave Starwood, that was evident. What had happened in the night was because of her. She couldn't think what she'd do or where she'd go, but she had to leave Joanne and her family before something worse happened than a rock through the window. She'd just sneak away, she didn't have the energy to argue with them.

She showered, stuffed her things in her suitcase, and went downstairs.

Breakfast was subdued.

Alex and Lily examined the plywood over the window and asked question after question about the broken window and who'd done it. Colin explained that it was probably just some bad guys playing a prank.

Luke called and asked if Harper would be ready to come in to the police station at nine. There was still a patrol car outside and Harper tried to figure a way she could leave without them seeing. There was a back alley, she'd go that way.

"Here's my cell number, Harper. You call if you need anything at all," Colin said.

"You have mine, I'm just a couple blocks away at the Library," Joanne added.

Soon everyone was gone, leaving Harper slumped at the table in the kitchen, trying to force herself to take action. Her ribs felt marginally better; she'd just swallowed a couple doses of the pain medication Colin had given her.

She thought of sweet Lily, her tiny body curled into Harper's arms in the night, almost as if the little girl knew how much she needed comforting. She felt like such a traitor, leaving everyone without saying goodbye, without thanking them for their generosity and kindness.

She was still trying to talk herself into grabbing her stuff and getting out of town when the doorbell rang.

Harper froze. "Who's there?" she called.

"Ma'am, it's Constable Erley."

Harper checked through the side window before

opening the door, and then she gasped when Quinn shouldered around the policeman and came in.

"What--what are *you* doing here? I don't want you here, so leave."

Quinn stood quietly, but his dark eyes reflected hurt and puzzlement. "Luke called, he told me what happened."

"Ma'am, Mr. Valdez says you know him," the officer said.

"I'd like for you to arrest him, is what I'd like," Harper said, keeping her eyes on Quinn.

"Can you please explain to me what's going on here, Harper?" Quinn raised his voice. "Why did you tell Luke it was me who caused this?"

"Stay here," Harper ordered the officer and then she pulled Quinn into the house, leaving the door wide open.

"How dare you come here after what you did?" she hissed at him.

"Harper, what are you talking about? Didn't we agree I'd come help you if you had any trouble? And I told you I'd never breathe a word about you being here."

"That was before you let Brad know where I was," Harper said. She felt dizzy and sick, remembering how she'd trusted him, how she'd been powerfully attracted to him. Even now he sounded so convincing.

She leaned back against the wall, rubbing her arms with her hands, staring at him. He was so physically attractive, tall and trim and strong. How could looks be so deceiving?

His dark eyes appeared to be genuinely confused. How could he be so different inside, so devious? The sense of betrayal hurt more than the physical pain in her body.

"Let this Brad know—you've got to be kidding." Quinn scowled at her. "I told you, I've never met this Brad character. So, you think he's the one who did this?" He waved a hand at the boarded-up window.

"Him or one of his lackeys. And don't play dumb," Harper shrieked. She felt totally out of control, defeated, furious. "What's he got on you, Quinn? Joanne said you were raising your sister all by yourself, so he probably what? Loaned you some money? I know all about that, that's what he did to me. And you *lied*, to me, to Joanne—you put her kids in danger."

"Stop right there. Not another word of this garbage." Quinn took two steps towards her and Joanne flinched, holding her hands up in a defensive pose.

He looked shocked at her reaction. He shook his head, held up his own hands, palm out. "My God. I'm not about to hurt you, I'd never hurt you. But get this through your head, I didn't lie to you or Joanne. I have no idea who this Brad character is, but it sounds as if he's bad news. And just so you know, I raised my sister with honest money, money I earned by working hard. I'd never do anything to endanger anyone, least of all Joanne and Colin and the kids. Or you, Harper."

He sounded so plausible. Joanne searched his face, his tone of voice, for anything that didn't ring true. And a tiny bit of uncertainty wormed its way into her. Could she be wrong about Quinn?

His voice softened. "I understand you're scared, sweetheart. I would be too if someone had turned me black and blue, threatened me, followed me and smashed windows. That's the act of a bully, and bullies are always cowards. Now, could we shut the door and talk about this over a coffee?"

Harper thought it over and then nodded. He was right. Brad *was* a bully. She knew that. But a coward? She'd just never thought of him that way before. It took away some of his power for some reason.

Cowards were dangerous, but they weren't untouchable. She thought of how Brad always hung out with weak people he could take advantage of, the way he never antagonized big strong men, the way he laid blame on everyone else but never himself. Of course he was a coward, Quinn was absolutely right. Why had she never recognized it herself?

Quinn said something to the cop, shut the door and came back over to her, taking her arm gently and leading her over to the table. He put out two mugs, poured coffee and sat down.

Harper tried to make sense of it all. "But—but if it wasn't you—I haven't talked to or seen anyone else since I got here. So how did he find out?" She knew she sounded hysterical. "How did he know I was staying with Joanne?"

Quinn put cream and two sugars in her cup and handed it to her. "Here, drink this. Not as good as tea, but it'll help."

She did as he suggested, and the hot, sweet liquid did help. She drew in a shaky breath.

"Someone found out," Quinn said. "Someone else had to have seen you. You came in by shuttle bus, right?"

And just like that, Harper knew what had happened. She gasped and put a hand over her mouth. "That bus driver. He kept talking to me, asking why I was coming to Starwood. He saw Joanne pick me up." How could she have forgotten?

Quinn nodded. "It wouldn't take much to find out where she lives. It's a small town, everyone knows Joanne because of the daycare."

"Quinn, omigod, I'm so very sorry." She felt a wave of hot shame wash through her. She'd jumped to conclusions, the wrong conclusions. "I—oh lord, Quinn, I told the cops it was you, that I was sure it was you." She felt horrified at what she'd done.

She was shocked when Quinn laughed and shook his head.

"Luke knows me. He knows I wouldn't do anything like that." He sobered and then held out his hand. "Let's go and find him, so you can tell him about the bus driver. And you also should lay assault charges against this Brad idiot."

Until that moment, she'd been certain she couldn't go through with it. But now she knew she could. She knew she *had* to. She nodded at Quinn.

He used his cell phone while she grabbed her handbag, and then she followed him out the door, squinting in the bright autumn sunlight. It seemed as if weeks had gone by since she'd last been outside, but it had only been just over a day.

Fear had turned her into a prisoner, a victim. She straightened her shoulders and vowed that she'd never let that happen again.

Quinn's battered half-ton truck was parked just across the street, and he held the door open for her. Sitting beside him, Harper was painfully aware of the physical attraction between them, and the mess she'd made of things by accusing him,

At the RCMP office, Luke was waiting for them.

"I—I made a bad mistake, accusing Quinn," Harper blurted out. "I've figured out who it was, who saw me."

Luke nodded. He greeted Quinn like an old friend, and then turned to Harper.

"Do you have any objections to Quinn sitting in on this? He's an auxiliary member of the Force, I'd like him briefed."

Shocked, Harper turned to Quinn. "Why didn't you tell me you worked with the police?"

"I wanted you to come to your own conclusions about me."

Luke took them into a small room. "Would you consent to having a female constable photograph your bruises, Harper?"

Harper grimaced and then shook her head. She'd been afraid this would be part of the process. It made her uncomfortable, but she knew it was also necessary. She also agreed to let the RCMP have access to Colin's medical records, if there were any.

A young female constable named Smithers took her into the women's bathroom. Harper took off her shirt and pulled her jeans down below her hips.

Smithers snapped photos of her bruised body. "My aunt Elaine was with a guy who knocked her around," Smithers said with a sigh. "I hope we nail the creep that did this to you."

"Not as much as I do," Harper sighed, putting her clothes on again.

Back in the interview room, Luke turned on the tape.

Luke asked questions and listened closely as she related the details of the beating she'd sustained from Brad, the new information about the bus driver, and everything she knew about the drugs and trafficking of women with which Brad was involved.

Luke gave quiet orders to Smithers locating the shuttle driver.

Quinn said nothing, but his jaw tensed and his hands tightened into fists when Harper described the assault.

Luke said, "Are there any witnesses to what he did to you?"

Harper nodded. "Two women. But I'm sure they'll be too scared to say anything. He said he was teaching them a lesson, that that's what would happen to them if they crossed him."

"We'd like to try to contact them. Could you give me their names?"

Harper hesitated. She didn't want to bring trouble down on the women, but if no one did anything, they could likely be the next ones Brad beat on. And how long before he ended up killing someone?

"Marlene Draper and Judy Wills. Judy worked for me as a bartender for a while."

"Do you have addresses for them?"

"They're living at Brad's house." She recited the address.

"We need to get a restraining order on Blackwell which prevents him from coming anywhere near you or your home or your place of business," Luke said.

Harper sighed. "He has guys who work for him. He'll just send one of them."

"Then we include all of them in the order. Do you have their names?"

"Most of them."

He wrote them down. He asked more questions and Harper answered as well as she could.

"Will you be willing to go to court and testify against Blackwell?"

Harper realized how far she'd come when she said with firm conviction, "Yes, I will."

When the interview was over, a secretary came in with a transcript of what Harper had said.

Harper stared at it for a long moment. Signing it would mean there was no way back. It would mean Brad Blackwell would do his best to destroy her.

Or it could mean that he would never be able to terrorize any woman again.

She reached for a pen and scrawled her name in bold letters.

Luke asked several more questions, then thanked Harper for the information.

"I've spoken with Inspector Biggs at the Calgary detachment," Luke said. "Brad Blackwell is very much a person of interest to them. They're aware of his involvement in drugs and prostitution. I'm convinced, based on your statement, that there's enough evidence to recommend to Crown Council that assault charges be laid against him. A warrant will then be issued for his arrest."

Harper swallowed hard. "How long will that take? Because I need to go back to Calgary and run my business, but I'm afraid of what he might do." Afraid, yes. Terrified, no. Harper recognized the difference.

"I can't promise anything, but my guess is that this shouldn't take longer than a day. I'll let you know the moment I hear."

"What—what about the money I owe him?" She reiterated how Brad had added on exorbitant interest, how he came by the bar and simply cleaned out the cash drawer.

"You need a good lawyer." Luke scribbled on a piece of paper and handed it to Harper. "Jane's handled several things for my wife and me. She's excellent. And Quinn knows her as well."

"Thank you." *Jane Shepard*, he'd scrawled, along with a phone number. She tucked the paper in her pocket.

There was more to talk to a lawyer about than just the money she owed, the secret that no one knew. The old familiar ache in her chest made her press a hand against her heart. She knew what she had to do but knowing didn't make it any easier.

Luke got up and he and Quinn escorted Harper back to the outer office. She felt drained and exhausted, but in a good way.

Quinn said, "Could I have a word, Luke?" They stepped into a room and shut the door. Harper sat down and waited, curious about what was being said.

After a few moments, Quinn came out, helped her to her feet and led the way to the truck. Again, he held the door while Harper got in.

He had lovely old-fashioned manners, and she loved that about him. She tried to remember when anyone had treated her like a lady before and came up blank. It was such a shame she'd ruined things between them with her accusations, but it was also foolish to think in terms of an on-going relationship. Maybe it was best this way.

"Now that that's out of the way and you're officially out of hiding, how about us having lunch somewhere?" Quinn settled behind the wheel and waited for her to answer.

Harper stared at him. "You're asking me out after what I did to you?"

He smiled at her. He had a great smile, wide and open. It included his eyes, such dark, lovely eyes.

"You're an interesting woman, Harper. Dangerous, for sure. But I always liked a touch of danger. It keeps life interesting." He started the truck. "So, lunch? I know a great place."

Remnants of fear still lurked inside of her. But she'd done the thing she'd been most afraid of—turning Brad into the cops. It was time to start living her life again.

"Okay. I'd like to go for lunch." She was actually hungry. And she wanted to find out more about Quinn. She was still shocked at finding out he worked for the RCMP. What other secrets was he hiding?

Probably nothing like the one that felt like a stone in her heart.

4

The Biggest Little Truckstop was obviously a happening place.

Harper knew that Starwood advertised itself as home of The World's Biggest Truck. The monstrous thing sat in the centre of an open lot like something out of a kid's movie, dwarfing the tourists gathered all around it taking photos.

And someone brilliant had capitalized on it and started a diner next to it. Within walking distance was the Library, where Joanne had her daycare.

Quinn escorted her into the café. The place was noisy and full, the smell's intoxicating. It felt inviting and friendly. Western music played. A pretty waitress with pink hair, noticeably pregnant, smiled and waved at them.

Harper paused just inside the door, taking in the décor. A big wooden sign on the wall said, "SIT LONG, TALK MUCH, EAT LOTS."

A huge blackboard announced the daily specials, *Pik-Axe Pasties, Blaster's Soup, Coal-Car Charlie's Stew, Maisie's Cheesecake, PickN'Shovel Pie. Try Our All-Day Breakfast.*

"Hey Quinn, there's a table for two at the back by the window," the waitress called, deftly serving loaded plates of food for a table of eight.

"Thanks Stella." Quinn led the way to the small table, half hidden by a gigantic pot of sunflowers.

"Wow, this is an amazing place. Especially for a small town." Harper was staring around, admiring the original wildlife art on the walls, the efficient way the waitress served, cleared, greeted customers. She felt a pang of envy.

"I'd love to add great pub food at the Whiskey-Jack, paint the walls, put up some art. Maybe if Brad's out of the picture—"

"You said you owed him money?"

Harper nodded. "Yeah. I've paid off a lot of it, but he keeps adding on interest."

"You've kept records of how much you've paid?"

"Of course."

"Like Luke said, you need a lawyer. Why don't you give Jane Shepard a call? I'll drive you over there after lunch if she has time to see you."

Things were moving almost too fast. Harper dug her cell phone out. A friendly male voice said that Ms. Shepard had an opening at one-thirty.

Harper confirmed the appointment just as the waitress came to take their order.

"Stella Montague, this is Harper Goodman," Quinn said.

Stella handed them menus and then reached out a hand and shook Harper's. "Welcome to the Biggest Little," she said with a wide smile. "You just visiting, Harper?"

A short time ago, she'd have been convinced that Stella was a spy for Brad. Harper realized now just how paranoid she'd been.

"Yeah, just visiting." It had been a pretty tumultuous visit, too.

"Quinn, you decided yet whether you're going fishing with Chad next weekend? Because if you're not, I'll get the paint for the baby's room."

"Not going to be able to make it," Quinn said. "Something's come up." His eyes twinkled with mischief. "Really sorry to let you down, Stella. I know you were counting on him being away."

She punched his shoulder and held two thumbs up. "*Yeeessss,*" she squealed. "Now he's got no excuse."

Quinn laughed. "Stella's married to a friend of mine, Constable Chad Montague," he explained to Harper. "Strangely enough, he'd rather fish than paint."

"Ain't that the truth," Stella drawled. "Now, what can I get for you?"

Intrigued by the catchy names, Harper ordered pasties and soup. Quinn opted for the stew.

The food was delicious. For a few moments they ate in silence. Then Harper took a sip of her mineral water and looked into his eyes. "So, who are you really, Quinn Valdez?"

He gave her a questioning look. "What do you mean? You know I'm a carpenter."

"And a cop, I didn't know that. So how many other personalities are you hiding?"

"That's it. What you see is what you get." He shook his head. "And I'm not a cop, just auxiliary. Sort of an assistant."

"What made you decide to be an auxiliary?"

"I was in the army. I had the right training. Luke needed someone from the area who knew the locals."

"Joanne said you'd been married." She was being downright nosy here, but he'd heard all her private stuff today at the cop shop. So she had a right, didn't she? She suddenly had an insatiable urge to know all about this man.

"I was. It seems a long time ago now. I met her while I was in the army, in Ontario. Laura was a nurse. She loved the city, so when my mom died and I decided to come back here to care for Lucy, she didn't want to move." He grimaced. "Things had been falling apart anyhow, we wanted different things. She re-married shortly after we divorced, to a psychiatrist. They have two kids now."

"You want kids someday?" It wasn't at all what she'd been planning to say.

He gave her a curious look. "I do. I'd like a big family someday soon. How about you, Harper?"

She shook her head, and a cold fist seemed to clutch at her heart. "Nope. My lifestyle isn't right for kids. I'd be a terrible mom."

"You never know until you try. I didn't know if I'd be able to take care of Lucy properly, but I found out not much matters as long as a kid has love. I mean, you have to provide a decent home, but kids don't care about stuff like fancy food or ironed clothes."

"Yeah." Her voice was bitter. "Ask any foster kid, they'll tell you that."

"Is that how you grew up, Harper? As a foster kid?"

"Yeah." She swallowed hard. "And not all foster parents are like Joanne and Colin."

"It was bad for you." It wasn't a question. "I'm really sorry." He leaned across the table and touched a gentle finger to the fading bruises around her eyes. "It's about time things changed for the better for you, sweetheart. You deserve some happiness in your life."

He'd called her sweetheart before. Whether or not he

meant the endearment, his words touched something old and wounded, deep inside of her.

Was she ever again going to get through a day without bawling? The tears trickled down her cheeks. Embarrassed, she sniffed and dipped her chin, hoping he wouldn't notice.

Of course, he did. He silently handed her some crumpled tissues, and she'd mopped her cheeks and blown her nose before Stella came back to ask about coffee and dessert.

"I'm full." Harper shook her head, but Quinn ordered Pick'N'Shovel Pie, with two forks.

"You gotta try this stuff, it's really good."

It was way beyond good, it was addictive. They shared the luscious caramel and chocolate concoction. They sipped the full-bodied coffee the diner had specially ground.

It was sensual and intimate, sharing bites of dessert, Quinn's hand brushing against hers. She tried to remember when she'd spent time just enjoying a quiet meal with a handsome guy and came up empty.

"I'm so full I won't be able to walk out of here," Harper sighed as Quinn fed her the last morsel of pie.

"I'll carry you then, because we have to get going if you're gonna make that appointment with Jane." Quinn paid the bill.

Stella said, "If you're still here on the weekend, Harper, get Quinn to bring you to the barn dance. Chad's off on Saturday and he's not fishing Sunday, so we'll be there."

"Thanks, I'll do that." Harper smiled at the friendly waitress, feeling a pang of regret. She'd be back in Calgary long before then.

The lawyer's office was a small storefront on the main street, and when Quinn pulled up in front of it, the relaxed ease of the past hour fled and a feeling of dread came over Harper.

Here it was. She'd do what she knew had to be done, but it didn't make it easy.

Quinn came in with her and introduced her to Jane, a tall, handsome woman with steel grey hair and a no-nonsense manner. Her face was wrinkled, lines of kindness and humor surrounding her mouth and her penetrating blue eyes. Her gaze lingered on the bruises on Harper's face.

Quinn said, "I've got some things to do, so just call my cell when you're done. I'll come get you." He left and Jane led the way into her cluttered office.

"What can I do for you, Harper?" Jane waved at a chair and Harper sank into it, staring at the green necklace Jane wore, wondering where to start.

Brad. He was the beginning, and, she prayed, the end.

"There's this guy I'm mixed up with," she blurted out, and from there on it was easy. Jane was a good listener, asking pertinent questions and jotting notes down on a pad, but not interrupting as Harper told her what she'd told the police. When she finished, she felt lighter, as though a heavy burden had dropped away.

"Luke feels confident there's enough evidence for crown counsel to issue an arrest warrant?"

"Yes. He thought probably later today. I also filled out the papers for a restraining order."

"Good." For the next hour, Jane quizzed Harper for details and outlined exactly what actions Harper should take regarding the debt to Brad.

"Is he named on the deed to the business as co-owner?"

"No." Brad had pressured her to do that, but for once she'd held firm.

Between bank statements and Harper's records, which

Harper was able to access on the office computer, Jane was sure the court would consider the debt paid in full.

It felt like a miracle. It felt like freedom. Harper drew in a breath that went all the way down to her belly.

Jane smiled at her, a wide, compassionate smile filled with warmth and support. "Now that's all settled, is there anything else we haven't covered?"

Harper hesitated, but only for a second. Over and above lawyer-client privilege, she knew she could trust Jane.

"Yes. Yes, there is." She drew in a shaky breath. "No one knows this, but I have a baby, a little girl. Emily." Harper's voice softened, speaking her daughter's name. "She's in foster care in Edmonton. She's four months old. Brad Blackwell was her sperm donor." She would never refer to him as Emily's father. Her hands were in her lap, and she squeezed her fingers into her palms so tight her nails dug into her skin.

"Does he know about Emily?"

"No." Harper's voice rose. "No, and he mustn't *ever* find out about her. No one knows except a social worker in Edmonton."

5

Harper's voice shook with emotion. "See, no one knew I was pregnant. I only started to show when I was six months along, and that's when I told everyone in Calgary that I was going to Toronto to take a bartending course. Instead I went to Edmonton. I rented a room, used a phony name and ID. I didn't even have a doctor. Emily was born in the emergency room at the hospital, I had to have an emergency C section." She remembered the awful trip in the taxi, the driver swearing because of all the blood on the seats, the pain that made her scream and writhe.

She remembered the controlled panic at the hospital because she was bleeding out. Then, nothing more until she came out of the anesthetic, and then they let her hold Emily close to her heart, her beautiful, perfect little girl.

She drew in a ragged breath. "I had her with me for three weeks, desperately trying to figure out a way to keep her, how I could possibly give her a good life." The anguish she'd felt when she realized she just couldn't was still fresh. "There just wasn't any way. You can't bring up a baby in a dive bar. And I couldn't let Brad know about her."

She'd seriously thought of giving Emily to Joanne, but by that time Joanne had already taken on the care of Zalika. It was before Colin and Joanne got together. Joanne was spending days at the Calgary hospital while the baby had heart surgery. She had Alex and Lily to care for as well, and she was a single mom.

There was no way Joanne could care for a newborn, no way social services would agree to her taking on yet another child. They'd likely take away her other foster kids. And also, Brad knew Joanne and Harper were friends. There was a chance he'd put two and two together.

"I have no relatives, I grew up in foster care myself, it was the last thing I wanted for Emily. But If Brad found out about her—" Harper shook her head and shuddered. "He's not on her birth certificate, he doesn't even know she exists. But if somehow he found out, he could insist on blood tests, apply for custody." She had nightmares about that. "He'd do that in a minute, because it would give him control of me."

Jane nodded, her eyes filled with compassion. "I see. So how can I help?"

Harper was silent for a long moment. "I need your advice. I've never released Emily for adoption. She's with a couple who love her very much and—" her breath hitched —"and they want to adopt her."

Joanne thought of Zalika, of Lily and Alex, of how much they were loved, of the insecurity Joanne and Colin felt about not being able to make Alex fully and legally their son.

Her own memories of being a foster child, never really belonging anywhere, were still fresh and painful even after all these years. And yet, the thought of signing away all her rights as Emily's mother made her nauseous. She loved her baby more than life itself.

"So, you want to know what I think the best choice is for you and for Emily." Jane's eyes were troubled.

"Yes. Please. I—I just can't seem to make a decision."

Jane hesitated and then said, "How would you feel if you gave her up and then met a man with a heart big enough to raise her as his own?"

"I'd never forgive myself." Harper swiped at the tears she hadn't realized till now were trickling down her cheeks.

"There are guys like that around," Jane said with a gentle smile.

She was right. Colin had welcomed Joanne's kids with open arms and a loving heart. The only other man Harper'd ever met who might be like that was Quinn. She saw his strong face in her mind. She was powerfully attracted to him, but she was damaged goods. She needed to remember that.

In spite of herself, Harper thought of his kindness, his generosity of spirit. He was a good man, the kind of man who'd likely love Emily Rose as his own.

But how would he, how would any man, feel about raising Brad's child? She'd seen the raw anger in Quinn's eyes when she told about the beating. And wouldn't she, Harper, always worry about Brad learning the truth?

It was impossible. Her tears flowed freely now, grief at what could never be.

Jane handed her a box of tissues. "My advice when an important decision needs making is to give it some time." She reached across and patted Harper's hand. "It sounds as if your baby's in a stable home, that she's loved and well cared for. Blackwell, I hope, is heading for jail. You're under extreme stress, Harper, and your body's trying to heal from severe injury. Now is not the time to make an irrevocable decision about anything."

Harper blew her nose and nodded. "That—that makes sense." It gave her a bone deep sense of relief to acknowledge that Jane was absolutely right.

She really *didn't* have to decide right now. Emily Rose was okay where she was.

"Give yourself time to heal. Come back in a month and we'll talk about this again."

"I will. Thank you so much." The words were inadequate, considering what Jane had done for her. "How much do I owe you?"

"I'll bill you when the time comes, m'dear. For now, there's still a great deal that needs done regarding getting you free of your debt to Blackwell, I'll tend to that immediately. As for the rest, my advice is free. The washrooms just down the hall, if you'd like to freshen up before you call Quinn."

Harper did. She washed her flushed, tear-stained face and thought over what had happened today.

Contrary to her nature, she'd trusted Luke. She'd also trusted Jane. And she more than trusted Quinn. Trust had been so foreign to her nature, it seemed a miracle.

Nothing concrete had changed just yet, but it felt as if her life had somehow taken a turn for the better.

Ten minutes later, Quinn pulled up in front of the lawyer's office.

Harper had been watching for him, and she jumped into the truck before he had a chance to get out. She smiled at him.

He sat and looked at her before driving away. "Wow, pretty lady, you look a lot sunnier than you did before. It went well?"

"Really well. She's so good. So kind. I'm grateful to you and Luke for recommending her." She went on to tell him what Jane had said about the debt to Brad.

"And if she's right, Quinn, and I don't have to go on paying money out for nothing, omigod, I can start to do the things I've dreamed of at the pub, freshen the whole place up with paint and art, put in new bathrooms and a kitchen. I'll have to hire a cook, but having great food would attract a whole new kind of customer. I'm thinking maybe really good stuff like the Truckstop serves, some amazing desserts. Fantastic coffee, a wine list—" aware that she was babbling, she stopped and looked over at him. "Sorry, sorry. I'm being a motor mouth."

"Be my guest." His wide smile and teasing gaze told her he didn't mind at all. "I love seeing you like this, all excited about something good."

"It's just that I've lived scared for such a long, long while, and now I feel sort of free. I probably shouldn't get my hopes up too soon, though. Until I hear whether there's enough evidence to arrest Brad."

"If there is, are you planning to go back to Calgary right away?" He was navigating the busy streets back to Joanne's, not looking at her.

"Yeah. The guy who's running the place for me is someone I trust, not one of Brad's people. But he doesn't know about ordering supplies and he's not great at delegating. So stuff like clean up and staff scheduling gets missed. I really need to get back."

Quinn nodded. There was silence for several moments.

"I can finish the job I'm on, get Joanne's steps fixed for her. Then I'll come with you."

Harper gaped at him. "Come—come with me? To Calgary? Why—why would you do that, Quinn?"

"Luke and I agreed that it's a good idea for you to have some protection for at least a while, until everything shakes down and these thugs are either arrested or decide to relocate somewhere else."

"Like—like, you being my bodyguard?" She could *so* get used to that idea. "But—but why would you do that? Your business, your work with the police—your life is here."

He shrugged. "I'm self-employed, I can put off some of my contracted jobs for a while. I have a neighbor who'll look after my house. And Luke's okay with me being with you in Calgary as part of my auxiliary work."

Kindness wasn't a thing she was used to. From Joanne, yes, they were old friends. But Luke? And Quinn? She struggled with desperately wanting him with her and knowing it was a bad idea. "You—you hardly know me."

He pulled the truck up in front of Joanne's house and turned to her. "That's just it, Harper. I want to get to know you a whole lot better. Beginning now." He reached across the bench seat and drew her close. "Is that okay with you?"

Before she could say no, he pulled her into his arms and kissed her.

It was not the sort of kiss that demanded dominance or suggested ownership.

It was not the sort of kiss that led to the bedroom.

It felt almost like Quinn was pouring some of his soul into her in order to fill up the cracks in hers. But the cracks were deep. One kiss would not be nearly enough to fill them. It felt like crossing a bridge, but she had no idea where it was leading. Where it *could* lead.

Nowhere, Goodman. Get a grip.

There was no future for her with Quinn, she reminded herself. She had the huge secret of Emily, and secrets destroyed relationships.

But she pulled away from the kiss far too late. He was embedded in her heart, in her very soul, and now she was scared she'd never be able to forget him.

Her cell phone was ringing, and she was still breathing hard when she answered.

"Harper? It's Luke. You okay?"

"Yeah, I'm fine" she lied, because now her heart was hammering for an entirely different reason.

"I wanted you to know that crown council ordered the immediate arrest of Blackwell on charges of assault and battery. He's now in custody, and a search warrant is being implemented for his vehicles and his property. He was in possession of cocaine when he was apprehended, which was a lucky break for us."

A sigh that came from her toes and a choked sob were all Harper could manage.

"And the man who drove the shuttle bus is also in custody. We picked him up on an old warrant for possession, and when he realized he was facing jail time, he told us about pitching the rock through the window for Blackwell. We'll keep you posted on him and on Blackwell." Luke hung up. Quinn gave her a questioning look.

"They—they've arrested him, Quinn. And the guy who drove the shuttle, too. He confessed to throwing the rock through Joanne's window. And that he was working for Brad."

"Damned good thing," Quinn growled. "Scumbags like him and Blackwell deserve everything the law can throw at them."

"So. I'll be going back to Calgary tomorrow." She was both relieved and anxious. And sad. There were so many things about Starwood she was going to miss, beginning with the man beside her.

"If you can wait until afternoon, I'll drive you. I want to just get Joanne's stairs fixed before I take off."

This was where she should say no. This was where she ought to end this thing before it went any further. "I think that's a bad idea," was all she could manage.

"Why's that?"

"I can't—I don't want to—it's not a good idea for me to get involved with anybody right now."

"I'm not proposing marriage, sweetheart. Not yet. I'm just offering you a ride to Calgary." He started the truck again. "We'll discuss it later. Right now let's go tell Joanne the good news."

It was only a short drive to the Library. Quinn led the way down the rickety stairs to the area Joanne rented. "Gonna fix these suckers," Quinn muttered, testing the railing and shaking his head when it yielded. He opened the door to a large, brightly painted room.

Laughter, kid's shrill voices all talking at once, a baby crying and a man's deep voice singing *When You're Happy And You Know It* assailed their ears.

Harper stopped just inside the door, looking at all the kids. A few hours ago, seeing all these beautiful little people would have hurt unbearably, bringing up images of Emily and the decision she still had to make.

Somehow, Jane's advice had eased the pain in her heart. Nothing had really changed; she'd have to decide sooner rather than later what to do about her baby. Just not today, and that made everything easier.

Quinn headed over to the guy singing. He was sitting on a bean bag chair holding a small girl on one knee.

Harper glanced at him, and then looked again. He was wearing knee length shorts and he was missing one leg. He had a space age prosthesis strapped on a stump that ended just above his right knee.

"Harper, welcome to bedlam." Joanne, a baby on each hip, came out of a door that led to a bathroom. "Diaper duty," she said, wrinkling her nose and putting Zalika and the other baby into a huge playpen. "Come and meet Timothy. Hey Quinn, great of you to drop by."

Quinn was now on all fours on the floor. A boy was riding on his back as if he was a horse. He pretended to buck and the boy screamed with delight, hanging on to his shirt and grabbing for his hair.

It was obvious how much he liked kids. Harper felt a sharp stab of regret, a painful reminder of the future she dared not even dream about, the huge secret she was keeping from Quinn, the reason she couldn't let this thing between them go much further.

Timothy swung deftly to his feet as Joanne introduced them, balancing the little girl on his shoulders. "Pleased to meet you, Harper."

"Tim, hold the fort while Harper and I make a fresh pot of coffee, would ya?" Joanne led the way to a small kitchen area at the back where she turned to Harper, eyes dancing with excitement behind her red glasses. "Okay, spill. What's going on? I see you and Quinn got straight, how did that happen?"

Harper told her about the bus driver, about swearing out a complaint, seeing the lawyer, and the call from Luke about the arrests.

Joanne threw her arms around Harper. "I'm *so* proud of you for laying charges. I know how much courage that took. And getting out from under him with the money, that'll just be fabulous." She looked serious for a moment. "Do you think those creeps that work for Brad will leave you alone now?"

"Quinn insists he's coming back with me for a while to make sure nobody tries anything." Harper felt her face flush. "I didn't ask him, he volunteered. I guess he and Luke talked it over." She shook her head. "I can't let him do that, J-bird. He's got a life here, I'll have to be alone sooner or later anyway."

"If he and Luke think it's a good thing, don't fight it. I think it's a great idea." She laid a hand on Harper's arm. "Let people take care of you for a change, my friend. Relax a little, stop second guessing everything. I've told you, the Universe has a way of clearing the path if you just get out of the way. I know, it happened to me. Quinn's a great guy, he wouldn't be doing this if he didn't want to. And I doubt there's any way to stop him if he's got his mind made up. He's pretty stubborn."

"I'm so ashamed of myself for accusing him. He's—he's —honest." And so very, very much more. "I really wasn't thinking straight. I'm sorry."

"No harm done. We all knew it wasn't him. And he's a keeper." Joanne was filling the coffee carafe with water. "Don't be so hard on yourself, Harper. You've been through a horrible time. Colin's gonna be so pleased when I tell him how things are working out, he's been worried about you, too." She got out cups and a bowl of cut up fruit and veggies. "I'll give the kids snacks and juice, that'll settle them for maybe two minutes. If we're lucky, we can chug our coffee in peace."

"This is such a great place for kids, Joanne." Harper felt ashamed for not having asked Joanne more about her business. She'd been self centred, entirely focussed on her own problems. "Did you do all the decorating? It's so colorful and cheerful. It's fun."

"Thank you for the fun part, that's exactly what I'm aiming for. It's going really well, I had a waiting list, but I was able to take four more kids when I hired Timothy full time. He's a gem, fantastic with the little ones. He'd been working part time because his old prosthesis just wasn't much good. But he got this new one a month ago, and it's great. He's here full time now, it's like a miracle, having another body around all day."

"How did he lose his leg?"

"Motorcycle accident. And the crazy guy still rides with his new prosthesis. His Harley's out back."

They carried the coffee out. The men were now on the floor, building towers with huge lego blocks and letting the delighted kids knock them down.

Joanne gathered the little ones around a low round table, handing out juice boxes and fruit snacks while Harper served the coffee.

"I want to come in early tomorrow morning, like at 6, to repair those stairs," Quinn told Joanne.

"And I'll be going back to Calgary tomorrow," Harper said. "I can't thank you and Colin enough for taking me in." Her eyes met Quinn's. His were questioning.

"I'll be leaving in the afternoon, if that's okay with you, J-bird," she said after a long moment.

"Of course," Joanne said. "We'd love it if you stayed a week or two, but I know you need to get home. Just promise you'll come back for a proper visit really soon."

"I promise."

Quinn gave her a little, satisfied nod and a thumbs up.

Harper looked around, at Joanne, at Quinn. Just how far could she take this trust thing? Was it like a strong elastic band, able to expand even after it seemed stretched to the limit?

She drank her coffee, and when one of the babies started to cry, she went over and picked her up, cradling the warm, fragrant bundle next to her heart, thinking of her own baby girl.

"Trust me, my sweet Emily," she whispered into one tiny ear. *"Trust me to do my very best for you. If that means giving you up, it will break my heart, but I'll do it. Know that if I can find another way, I'll find it. Because I love you."*

Quinn couldn't have known what she saying, but he was watching her, and he got up and came over, touching a finger to the baby's back. He bent and pressed a gentle kiss on the downy head. "Babies. You look at them and you sort of know that anything's possible."

Harper looked up at him, at the warmth and kindness in his face, the softness in his eyes as he smiled down at the bundle she held. And she knew between one heartbeat and the next that he was right.

With love, anything was possible.

"That's got it, no more leaks." Quinn wriggled out from under the sink and got to his feet, turning on the faucet and crouching down to view his handiwork. "Dry as old Elmer's farts," he pronounced with a satisfied grin.

"What would I do without you?" Harper looked around at the shiny commercial kitchen. She couldn't stop smiling, and excitement rose inside of her like soap bubbles.

Quinn came up behind her and wrapped his arms around her in a bear hug. "I'm indispensable, and don't you forget it, sweetheart."

It was nothing less than the truth. She couldn't have come this far without him, and she was amazed and grateful, and so in love with him. They were partners in every sense of the word, and soon they'd legally be a couple.

He trailed a line of teasing kisses up and down her neck, and Harper turned around, pulled his head down, and kissed him properly. Being in his arms sent delicious shivers up and down her body. Strong hands, exploring lips, the smell of sawdust and pine and the cement he'd used on the pipes—all mingled with the intimate, masculine scent that was his alone.

"Not getting the urge to run away before the big day, are you, sweetheart?"

"The wedding? Or the grand opening?"

"Either or," he grinned.

"Not today," she teased. "Ask me again tomorrow."

Their wedding was planned for June. It was only March, yet already Joanne and the new female friends Harper had made since moving to Starwood were all up to their elbows planning the celebration. It seemed weddings in Starwood were community affairs.

It made Harper decidedly nervous, all the talk about decorations for the hall, invitations--*ribbons* for the church pews, for heaven's sake? She thought that tomorrow would be way less stressful than the wedding, even though it was the grand opening of the Old School Bar and Grill.

Tomorrow was the culmination of months of hard work, huge changes, emotional turmoil. And miracles, she couldn't discount miracles.

"You know I love you, sweetheart." Quinn nipped at her ear, and they were still holding each other when the back door opened and the chef she'd hired, Benny Laslo, came in carrying a huge plastic tub. He glanced at them and turned red.

Harper had noticed that any open display of affection embarrassed Benny—which was exactly why Quinn mischievously held on to her and thoroughly kissed her again, bending her back in his arms.

"Hey Benny," she managed to gasp, pushing Quinn away and mock frowning at him. "Are there more tubs in the van that need brought in? Quinn'll be happy to get them."

Quinn gave her a martyred look which she ignored.

"Yeah, five more. I've got all the non-perishables for tomorrow. And Mac says if I forget anything, they'll send it over from the Truckstop. They're also supplying all the desserts for the party."

"That's so good of them." Harper had become good friends with Mac Ferguson and his wife, Kate, the owners of the Truckstop. There was no hint of competition between her new business and theirs; the Bar and Grill was primarily a drinking destination, with a wide selection of local craft beer and good plain pub-food as a side benefit, with honey mustard wings for fifty cents offered four times a week, along with home-made fries. The Truckstop's menu was much more varied and elaborate.

Kate and Joanne had been more than generous with decorating ideas. It was Kate that had suggested the ad slogan—*OLD SCHOOL PUB WITH A MODERN TWIST.* The building *had* been a school years ago, then a storage site for mine supplies, and more recently a garage. And now it was Harper's dream come true.

It was Joanne who'd found the dozens of dark brown chairs that seemed to wrap a body in welcoming arms. They'd been rescued from the basement of the Black Nugget Hotel, and they'd cost a whopping twenty-five dollars each.

The round oak tables had come from an old bar in Fernie that was shutting its doors after seventy years of business. They were solid but scarred and carved and dirty. After Quinn cleaned, refinished and polished them, they were a lovely light gold, with marks that added character.

Harper walked out of the kitchen into the business area, trying to assess it from a customer's point of view.

The main room was large, open and inviting, with booths along the walls by the windows, the round oak tables arranged around two large pool tables. Huge black and white posters of early mining days and grizzled miners covered the old red brick walls. A giant stand-alone wood-burning fireplace was circled by plushy armchairs and two extra-long couches upholstered in a deep burgundy.

She gazed around, still hardly able to believe they'd pulled this off, her and Quinn. Moving to Starwood had marked the beginning of a blessed time in her life. She sank down on one of the comfy brown armchairs, remembering how it had all happened.

She'd realized soon after she went back to Calgary that in spite of Brad's arrest and probable conviction, she'd never truly relax again or enjoy running the Whiskey-Jack. There were too many bad memories, too many reminders of bad times.

Some of Brad's thugs had been arrested along with him, but a few hung around despite Quinn's protective presence. They didn't try anything, but knowing they were hovering was like a dark, ominous cloud.

After a few weeks, and after endless late-night pillow-talks with Quinn, she'd put the property and the business up for sale. To her amazement, she had an offer within a week for the full asking price the realtor had suggested, more money than Harper ever dreamed of having. A developer wanted the property for low rent condos.

"Let's move to Starwood," she'd blurted that night, amazed at what had just come out of her mouth. She was a city girl, wasn't she?

But Quinn's life was in Starwood, his carpentry business, his house, his work with the RCMP; he'd put it all on hold for her, a gesture that amazed and humbled Harper, and, if it was possible, made her love him all the more.

She realized she really liked the little town, and she

loved Joanne and Colin and the kids. It would be great to live close to them.

When Quinn mentioned that Starwood could do with a decent pub and told her of the old brick school that had been for sale for over a year, Harper got shivers down her back.

They'd driven through to Starwood, viewed the property, and she immediately recognized the potential. She'd made a low-ball offer that very day and it was accepted.

Quinn said that he'd do the renovations and pay for them, and when he'd insisted, Harper had secretly gone to Jane to draw up the terms of a tentative partnership, even though Quinn said the pub was hers alone.

"Have you told him about the baby?" Jane was nothing if not forthright.

Suddenly miserable and guilty, Harper shook her head.

"I've known Quinn since he was a youngster. He's an unusual man, Harper. I can see that you care for him, and it's obvious he loves you. Give him a chance, why don't you? Trust him. He's a very loving guy, I know because of the way he was with Lucy, his little sister. And with Blackwell facing serious charges of assault, possession and trafficking, I think he'll be unlikely to bother you. He's heading to prison for a nice long visit. No judge in their right mind would pay any attention to a custody request from him, should he ever make one."

So it was on the drive back to Calgary that weekend that she'd finally told Quinn about Emily. They loved one another, and now they were also business partners, but there's always been this one hurdle she couldn't cross. As Jane had reminded her, their relationship had to be based on truth and trust, but it was so hard to say the words that needed said.

She knew she was gambling everything. She'd wrapped her hands tight around her belly, and her voice quavered. She didn't look at him. Instead she stared out the window at the prairie landscape flying past as she blurted it all out, the secret she'd held for so long.

"Remember when you asked me about the scar on my stomach, Quinn? I-I lied to you, I said it was a botched appendix operation. The—the truth is, it was from a caesarian." She gulped and forced herself to go on. "I---I have a baby, Quinn. A little girl, Emily. I—I got pregnant by Blackwell. She's nine months old now, in—in a good foster home in Edmonton."

She'd stumbled on, spilling everything out, and he'd listened without saying a single word, just steering the pickup down the road, staring straight ahead.

"I—I've been terrified Brad would find out. He—he could try and take her from me. He doesn't know about her, but if he did—but Jane said I should stop worrying about that."

Her body got cold and then hot and she fought back tears, knowing she was losing the only man she'd ever truly loved. She couldn't look at him as she went on explaining why she'd kept the secret so long.

Suddenly the truck veered to the shoulder and jerked to an abrupt stop.

Harper braced herself on the dash, her stomach doing cartwheels. Was he going to tell her to get out, here in the middle of nowhere? It was no more than she deserved. She undid her seat belt, reached for the door.

In one lunge he closed the distance between them. His arms went around her, holding her painfully tight. His face was wet, and she realized he was crying.

"Let's go get her, sweetheart. Right away. Let's bring her

home." His lips closed on hers, and all of her doubts and fears evaporated with the intensity of his kiss.

When she could think again, she whispered, "Is it going to bother you, that genetically she's Blackwell's—"

"Listen to me." Quinn took her face between his calloused palms, his deep voice intense. "I told you my father was an abusive drunk who beat my mother. That doesn't mean I'm like him even if I have his genes. That doesn't mean my sister was like him. A baby is a baby, Emily will be my daughter in every way that matters. I'll love her because she's yours, because she's a little baby, because babies are miracles. I'll make her mine, I'll love her always. I promise."

It took two weeks of paperwork, but one sunny day she and Quinn drove to Edmonton and brought their daughter home. Her foster parents were sad to see Emily go, but Harper had promised visits and followed up on them. She sent photos every week, and now the loving couple was in the process of adopting a baby boy.

And Quinn was adopting Emily, so she could legally bear his name. She had him wrapped around her pudgy fingers to such an extent that Harper could almost feel jealous. Almost. If she wasn't so totally in love with both of them.

"Hey, lazybones, let's go pick the kid up and I'll take both my ladies for dinner at the Truckstop."

Emily was at the daycare with Joanne this afternoon. Normally, they kept her with them, but today they'd both been too busy, and Joanne and the older kids at the daycare adored having her visit.

Outside, the early spring day was already fading into night. Streetlights were on, and the little town looked snug and warm and welcoming.

Starwood, her town.

Quinn, her man.

Emily, their daughter.

Harper had been lost for so long, but finally she'd come home.

~

AFTERWORD

Starwood is the setting for **Starwood Chronicles**, a series of short exciting reads about the fun people who lead their lives in a little coal mining town in shadow of the Rocky Mountains.

The first four in the series are:

BIGGEST LITTLE TRUCKSTOP

EVERY LITTLE THING

BIGGEST LITTLE MUSTACHE

BIGGEST LITTLE HEART

I hope you enjoy **Biggest Little Secret**

I'd be so grateful for a review on Amazon.

I'd also like to give you a free book, one from another series , DOCTOR 911, stories about doctors and hospitals, life and death—and, of course, love. You can get it here:

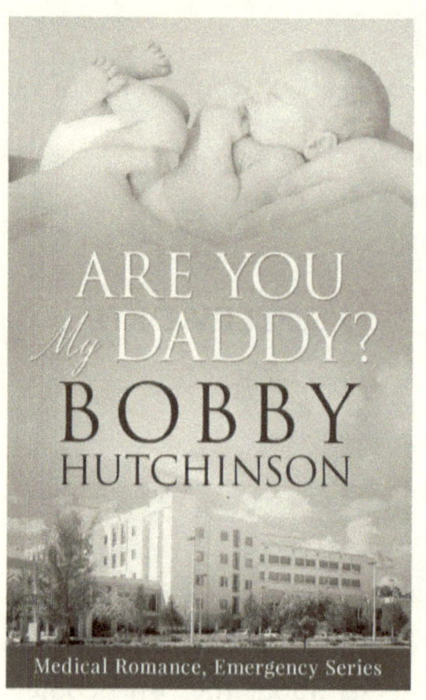

ARE YOU
My DADDY?
BOBBY
HUTCHINSON
Medical Romance, Emergency Series

ACUTE CARE

EIGHT BOOK MEDICAL BUNDLE:

EMERGENCY

ABOUT THE AUTHOR

Bobby Hutchinson lives, breathes, reads and writes books. She lives in a coal-mining town in the Rocky Mountains of B.C., Canada, a town remarkably like Starwood.

She isn't an RCMP officer, she doesn't waitress anymore, but she has fostered babies and she loves Irish doctors. She's never shot a stalker or owned a pub-but some of her wonderful female friends have done (most) of the above, which made for fantastic research in Biggest Little Secret.

Her favorite quote is, "When you change the way you look at a thing, the thing you look at changes."

9 798227 350978